WIlll   J

B̶̶̶s and Baubles

ALSO IN THIS SERIES

The Goffins

Bubbles and Baubles

JEANNE WILLIS

illustrated by **Nick Maland**

WALKER
BOOKS

This is a work of fiction. Names, characters, places and incidents are either the product of the author's imagination or, if real, are used fictitiously. All statements, activities, stunts, descriptions, information and material of any other kind contained herein are included for entertainment purposes only and should not be relied on for accuracy or replicated as they may result in injury.

First published 2012 by Walker Books Ltd
87 Vauxhall Walk, London SE11 5HJ

2 4 6 8 10 9 7 5 3 1

This book has been typeset in ITC Veljovic

Printed and bound in Great Britain by Clays Ltd, St Ives plc

British Library Cataloguing in Publication Data:
a catalogue record for this book is available from the British Library

ISBN 978-1-4063-2882-0

www.walker.co.uk

CONTENTS

THE CARRUTHERS

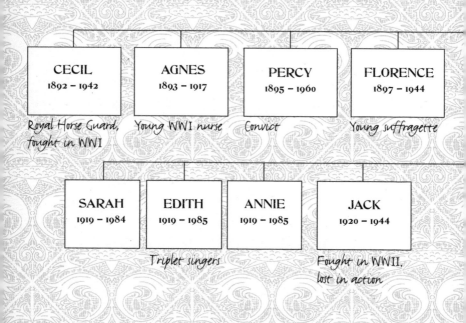

CECIL
1892 – 1942

Royal Horse Guard, fought in WWI

AGNES
1893 – 1917

Young WWI nurse

PERCY
1895 – 1960

Convict

FLORENCE
1897 – 1944

Young suffragette

SARAH
1919 – 1984

EDITH
1919 – 1985

ANNIE
1919 – 1985

Triplet singers

JACK
1920 – 1944

Fought in WWII, lost in action

FAMILY TREE

MONTAGUE CARRUTHERS
1870 – 1960
m
MAUD GOODWIN
1871 – 1971

Explorer, sailor, whaling ship

Suffragette, Titanic, WWI Nurse, maid servant called Violet, lived to be 100

SID
1899 – 1975
m
DOLLY GRAY
1900 – 1975

Joined army to fight WWI, under age, lost leg, won medals

VICTORIA
1901 – 1904

GORDON
1922 – 2005
m
PEGGY ELLIS
1926 –

Fought against Hitler in WWII as a young man

MARY
1926 – 2006

Evacuee

FRANK
1928 – 2003

Evacuee

SIMON
1958 –

PHILLIP
1960 –
m
SUSAN DERBYSHIRE
1966 –

Saved child from drowning

GEORGE
1999 –

Discovered Goffins living in his grandma's attic

THE STORY SO FAR...

George has a huge secret: there are Goffins living in his grandma's attic! Lofty and Eave belong to a race of people whose tiny island sank beneath the sea centuries ago. Homeless, their ancestors moved into the roofs of abandoned buildings, and now there are Goffins living in secret under every fifth roof in the country.

Like all Goffins, Lofty and Eave are skilled at recycling junk and have divided Grandma Peggy's attic into rooms furnished with bric-a-brac, stored there since Victorian times. Here, they survive on pigeon eggs, fruit from the roof garden, things Lofty fishes from Down Below, and any leftovers that George can sneak into the loft.

To his amazement, Eave knows more about George's family history than he does, from old letters and photos she has found. The more their friendship grows, the more George learns about Goffins, and the more he learns about himself...

CHAPTER ONE

TINSEL AND TIDIN'S

George only had two windows left to open on his advent calendar. It was almost Christmas – the best time of the year! But as George revealed a glittery picture of a sleigh, he sighed. For some reason he didn't feel the slightest bit Christmassy.

He couldn't understand it. When he was younger and lived in London, he used to get excited about Christmas Day as early as September, and would spend many an autumn evening drawing up a long list of presents for Father Christmas to bring. This year, George couldn't think of a single thing he wanted and that worried him.

Had he really changed that much since coming to live with Grandma Peggy and discovering Goffins living secretly in her attic? Maybe he had. As well as changing house and schools, he'd changed his mind about lots of things, thanks to Lofty and Eave. Seeing how they struggled to survive had made him realize how greedy and selfish he could be. Being the only one who knew they existed, he made it his daily duty to look after them.

George loved doing it and they were the best friends he could ever wish for, but it was a huge responsibility and he'd had to become far less lazy and a lot more thoughtful. Caring for the Goffins also had another side effect: it showed George just how much his mum and dad actually did for him. Horrified, he guessed that seeing things from their point of view could mean only one thing: he had grown up.

Did growing up mean he'd grown out of Christmas? George helped himself to a mince pie for breakfast in the hope that it would get him into the festive spirit, and wandered into the lounge. Rex followed behind him, polishing off the trail of pastry crumbs. Finding a

stray silk bauble under the Christmas tree, the dog barked with excitement, tossed it in the air and chased it round the carpet before dropping it in George's lap.

"Is that what you want for Christmas, Rex?" asked George, throwing the bauble back to his dog. "I don't know what I want any more."

11

Bubbies and Baubles

Everything was in place for a perfect
Christmas: the big box of baubles and
trimmings had been fetched from the
cellar; the tree was up; the fairy lights
worked. Every inch of the room
was bright with decorations – old
ones from George's childhood
mixed with even older ones from
Grandma Peggy's. So why did he
feel so flat?

Just then, his dad came into
the room with a packet of balloons. "Hey,
George. Want to give me a hand blowing up
these?" he asked. "Mum was going to but
she's not feeling too great at the moment."

"Is she throwing up again?" asked George.
He'd heard her in the bathroom when he
came downstairs. It had been going on for
days. "I hope I don't catch what she's got,"
he added.

"Oh, I don't think there's much chance of
that," smiled his dad.

George wasn't so sure. A lot of his friends had missed the end of term because of a nasty bout of winter flu. If he got ill and couldn't even eat his Christmas dinner it really would be the last straw.

"Mum will be fine," said his father, misreading George's worried expression for one of sympathy. "It's just one of those things. It'll pass."

"I expect she got it when she was working in the hospital," said George.

His father let go of the balloon he was blowing. It shot off round the lounge with a drawn-out farting sound and landed with a plop on top of the curtain pelmet. They both fell about laughing and for a few seconds George's mood started to lift – maybe Christmas was going to be good after all! But then his dad ruined everything.

"Stop it, George!" he guffawed. "We're a bit old to be going silly over a balloon, aren't we? Christmas is meant to be for kids."

George stopped laughing and sat up. "Is it?" His father had just confirmed his worst suspicions.

"Me and Mum used to love the letters you wrote to Father Christmas when you were little," he said. "But now you've started secondary school..." He trailed off and busied himself with another balloon, but George knew what he'd have said if he'd finished the sentence: now you've started secondary school you're too old to believe.

George felt his eyes prickle. His father must have noticed because he deliberately let go of another balloon, but this time George didn't find it funny.

Whether he believed in him or not, he'd still intended to write a letter to Father Christmas. He'd only put off doing it because he didn't know what he wanted. It was what he'd always done; it was as traditional as turkey – but it was for little children. Clearly his father didn't think he was one of those any more.

"I will still get presents though, won't I?" asked George.

His dad tied a knot in the neck of a balloon and batted it to Rex. "Of course you will. Just don't expect too much this year."

George couldn't see why. Usually he got loads of presents. Both his parents worked. It wasn't like they were poor.

"Why, have you lost your job, Dad?"

"No, we just need to watch the pennies a bit."

15

Bubbies and Baubles

George had been hoping that as he hadn't mentioned what he wanted, his parents would have put their heads together to surprise him with the perfect present. After all, it wasn't as if he had any brothers or sisters to buy for. If he was honest, though, he couldn't think of anything that would make his day unless it was a brand new car, which he wasn't old enough to drive anyway. Oh, please don't let it be a jumper, he prayed – especially not one knitted by Grandma. He wouldn't be able to hide his disappointment. George got up and left the room.

"Thought you were helping with these balloons," said his dad, somewhat deflated.

"I *hate* Christmas," groaned George. "I'm going to my room."

As he stomped up the three flights of stairs to his bedroom in the attic, he realized he sounded just like a stroppy teenager. He hadn't meant to – he was only eleven – but he didn't feel the same as he did when he was ten. He wasn't in the Juniors any more and although that was great in many ways, part of him wished he was still as young as Eave.

He decided to go and see her. Usually when he went to visit the Goffins, he took something for them: food to pad out the fruit and vegetables Eave grew in her roof garden, or something useful, like batteries, toothpaste or soap. The Goffins couldn't get these things for themselves because they didn't use money and rarely left the loft. They couldn't risk getting caught.

17

Bubbies and Baubles

Today, George arrived with a mince pie in each pocket. It wasn't much but it was all he'd been able to grab, what with his dad hanging around. He knocked softly on the small green door that led to the attic.

Pom ... tiddy pom pom ... pom pom!

Recognizing the code he'd used, Eave opened the door immediately, as if she'd been waiting for him for some time. She was dressed in a huge Russian hat, which she'd pulled down over her wild, copper hair, and an antique fur coat that billowed over a pair of sealskin boots that looked as if they'd once belonged to an Inuit with much larger feet than hers. She was dancing up and down on the spot like an over-excited bear cub.

"Jowge! Myneself be so gleefill. 'Tis most wonderful tidin's!"

She waved a letter at him and ushered
him into the loft. Being the middle of winter
it was cold in there – but the Goffins were a
very hardy race and a practical one. They had
no central heating so Lofty had lagged the
rafters with old carpets, rugs and newspaper
to exclude any draughts, and there was some
warmth to be had from the twelve candles in
the huge chandelier that lit the attic.

George stood under it and watched as Lofty balanced on a ladder, putting the final touches to the Christmas decorations. He'd turned the attic into a Yuletide grotto, swathing the beams in garlands and tinsel left in the loft by generations of George's ancestors, going right back to Victorian times.

Pinned to the walls among the hundreds of yellowing photos of his long-departed relatives were old Christmas cards that Eave had found among the memorabilia

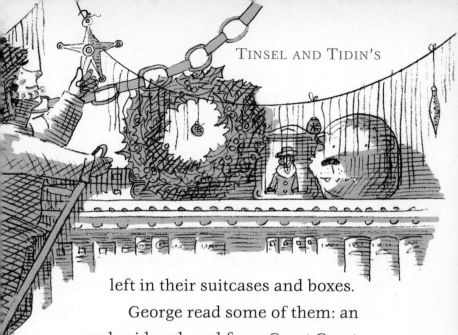

left in their suitcases and boxes.

George read some of them: an
embroidered card from Great-Great-
Grandma Maud to Great-Great-Grandpa
Montague. Another written in the trenches
from Great-Grandpa Sid to Great-Grandma
Dolly. Cards drawn with crayons from their
children Mary and Frank, who had been
evacuated to the countryside during WWII
just before the bombs started to fall.

Mary and Frank had been separated and
sent to live with different families, far away
from each other; George noticed there was
a different address in the corner of each
card. Mary had gone to Hereford and her

21

little brother Frank to Southend-on-Sea. George couldn't imagine how lonely and frightened they must have been, staying with complete strangers in an unfamiliar place without each other.

The messages they'd written inside the homemade Christmas cards to their parents were overly cheerful – the sort of letter a child might write when they were desperately homesick but had been told very strictly not to worry their family with their own woes. It brought a lump to George's throat. Although there were times when his parents drove him crazy, he couldn't imagine anything worse than spending Christmas without them.

"Jowge, yourself will never be guessin' what myneself be gettin' for Yuletide!" said Eave, interrupting his thoughts.

"Tell me."

George wasn't in the mood for guessing games so she gave him the letter she was holding. It was heavily creased from being folded small enough to be carried by her pet pigeon, Chimbley, but George recognized the address straight away. It had come from Granny Cloister's belfry where Eave's brother Arch and her mother, Ariel, lived. George squinted at the tiny writing.

"What? I don't believe it," he grinned. "Is this for real?"

"Yay! Myneself be havin' a new bubby sister!" squealed Eave, grabbing his hands and swinging him round.

By the proud look on Lofty's face, George knew it had to be true.

CHAPTER TWO

LOFTS AND LEAVING

According to the letter, Eave's baby sister had been born in the belfry last week.

"Us be callin' her Valley. Herself be weighin' six whole puddin's!" beamed Lofty, his mouth crammed with mince pie.

"Valley?" said George. "That's nice."

He forced a smile. He was trying hard to sound happy about the new baby but in truth he was jealous. He hated being an only child. When he was younger, he used to beg his mum to give him a brother or sister to play with, but he never got one.

When George first met Eave, she'd taken

him out onto the roof and they'd had a long talk up in the clouds. Realizing they were both lonely, she said she'd be his 'step-in' sister if he would be her 'step-in' brother, to make up for the fact that Arch was living somewhere else. She wasn't real family, but she was the closest George had ever come to having a sister. Now Eave had a brother and a sister – the full set – maybe she wouldn't need a step-in brother anymore.

George sat down sadly on the faded lilac chaise longue in the room that Eave called the parlour. It was piled high with old baby clothes she'd found in the loft: bonnets, bootees, impossibly small leather shoes that still bore the imprints of tiny toes. There was a doll-sized christening gown made of ivory silk.

George felt the fabric between his fingers.

"Whose baby sister did this belong to?" he wondered wistfully. Eave made a little space among the woolly things and sat down next to him.

"Jowgie, whyfor be yourself sorrowfill? 'Tis a merry time, nay?"

"I dunno, Eave. I'm just being silly," he said. "Take no notice of me. I think it's brilliant about your new sister. I really do…"

She peered from under the brim of her fur hat and fixed him with her gooseberry-green eyes. "Myneself be havin' a normous wish, Jowge."

He knew what was coming before the words were even out of her mouth.

27

"You want me to take you to see the baby," he guessed.

Eave flung her arms round his neck.

"Yay! Pappy? Did yourself be hearin'? Jowge be takin' us to see the bubby!"

George, who had no intention of doing any such thing pushed her away as gently as he could.

"I never said that. The last time I took you to visit your family it was a nightmare getting you there and back. And I'm sure Grandma Peggy saw you!"

George suspected that Grandma Peggy had known about the Goffins all along – but she'd never said anything and he'd never mentioned them to her. On the day he'd taken Lofty and Eave out and forgotten his key, Eave had had to break in through the window and Grandma Peggy had seen her. George had managed to convince Grandma she was dreaming, but it was a close call. He didn't want to go through that again.

"There's no way I can take you all the way to the belfry again," he said. "I'm sorry."

Eave looked at him with utter dismay, then she pulled her hat right down to her chin and began to sob, her tears muffled by the fur. George held out his hands in despair.

"*You* understand why we can't go, don't you, Lofty?"

Lofty nodded slowly. "Us do live in dread of bein' cotched," he said, trying to comfort Eave. "Us must bide by Jowge's judgemint, Littley. No matter! Us will be seein' Valley come springtimes."

Eave pushed back her hat and gave a little smile.

"Come springtimes, us be all to-gathered again, yay? Myneself, Muppy … Arch…"

George looked at her aghast.

"What are you talking about? You're not leaving, are you? You *can't*!"

Bubbies and Baubles

The Goffins exchanged awkward glances.
Lofty removed the black bearskin busby he
was wearing and sat down next to George.

"Ah, myneself has been meanin' to tell
yourself somethin', Jowge."

George put his hands over his ears.
He didn't want to hear what was coming.
He knew it might happen one day, but did
it have to be so soon?

"As yourself be knowin'," continued Lofty
softly, "Grandmuppy Cloister's place be most
smincey. There be no room to swirl a squill,
let alone a bubby."

George knew what a squeeze it was in the belfry. He'd stayed there once and seen for himself. The church bell took up so much space, there was barely room for Ariel, Arch and Granny Cloister, which is why Lofty and Eave had had to leave the others and move into Grandma Peggy's attic in the first place. Now the baby had arrived, it would be even more cramped there.

"Themselves must be movin' on," said Lofty, "and so must us. 'Tis time myne fambily be livin' under one roof."

George felt as if he'd been punched in the stomach.

"Can't they come and live here?" he pleaded, looking round at the odd bits of furniture that Lofty and Eave had used to create separate rooms. Beyond the parlour was a kitchen, a bathroom, two bedrooms and a tiny toilet. George tried to rearrange the layout of the attic in his head – there had to be a way of making it big enough for three extra Goffins and one tiny one.

"Maybe if we moved things around, we could fit everyone in. We could make a nursery for the baby. I can always bring more milk and..."

Lofty was shaking his head. "Nay, Jowge. Us can't be squeezin' a mammuth into a meecehole. 'Tis a wonderfill dream but even if us all be fittin' in, bubbies be howlin' and skrikin' most terribil loud. Us would be cotched afore sunsit."

George knew he was right but he couldn't bear the thought of life without Lofty and Eave. His friends at school weren't half as much fun as the Goffins. Who would he have to talk to when they were gone? Who would listen his troubles?

"Yourself and Rex can always be comin' to stay," said Eave. "Myne brother Arch will be findin' us a normous roof someplace. Himself be searchin' already most likelee."

"Will he?" asked George dully. "Already?"

They would probably move miles away. They were bound to – empty roof space was rare these days. The abandoned houses and derelict buildings near Grandma Peggy's were already occupied. "Yourself be never more than five roofs away from a Goffin," Lofty had told him.

"You're going *this* spring?" George mumbled. "That's not far off."

"Us will be havin' fun, yay?" said Eave brightly. "When yourself comes a-visitin'."

"Yeah," said George. "I s'pose."

He didn't want to be a guest though. He wanted to be George Carruthers, their hero, the one who looked after them. But they had survived without him long before he moved into Grandma Peggy's and they would do again, wherever they went. Begrudgingly, George realized that he needed the Goffins more than they needed him, and with that unhappy thought he said he'd see them later and went downstairs.

He bumped into his mother coming out of the bathroom. She looked just like he had the time he went on a ferry and threw up overboard. She didn't seem to notice how upset he was.

"Do me a favour, George," she said. "Take Grandma's lunch to her, please. She wants it in bed and I can't bear the smell of liver and onions at the moment."

She turned and went back into the bathroom, leaving George with no choice. He sloped off to the kitchen and found Grandma Peggy's lunch sitting on top of the cooker under some tin foil. Using a tea towel, he put the hot plate and a knife and fork on Grandma's tray with the fancy handles.

Hotly pursued by Rex, he took the tray down the hall to Grandma Peggy's room. Without thinking, he knocked on the door using the same code as he used for the Goffins.

Pom ... tiddy pom pom ... pom pom!

"Is that you, boy?" she called.

"No, it's Father Christmas."

He pushed the door open with his foot and went in. He hadn't meant to sound quite so sarcastic but Grandma gave as good as she got.

"Haven't you heard? 'Tis the season to be jolly," she said, putting her knitting down. "What's up with you, then? You've got that look on your face."

"No, I haven't," he said, grumpily.

"Yes, you have. Your Grandpa Gordon used to look like that when he was pretending not to be upset," she said, whipping the foil off her lunch.

"I hate Christmas!" blurted George. "I don't feel 'jolly' at all."

"I hate liver," said Grandma Peggy, throwing a piece to Rex. "What's really eating you, boy?"

He wished he could tell her the truth – that the Goffins were going to leave – but he couldn't. He'd promised Lofty and Eave he would never tell a soul they existed.

"Some really close friends of mine are moving away," he said, looking mournfully up at the roof through the French windows. Grandma noticed where his gaze fell and for a split second her expression faltered. She put down her knife and fork.

"There's a new baby in the family," added George. "They need a bigger place."

"Which family?" asked Grandma Peggy.

"The Lofthausens," said George, slightly too quickly.

A while back, he'd invented an imaginary friend called Hans Lofthausen to explain away an adventure with the Goffins. He'd embellished the lie so well, his mother had even sent the Lofthausens a Christmas card.

"Ah, the Lofthausens," said Grandma. "I never did meet Hans, did I? Don't suppose I ever will now if he's moving. Is he going back to Germany?"

"Yes, Berlin. Why do things have to change, Grandma? I liked things the way they were."

She pushed the fried onions onto the side of her plate and leant back on her pillow. "I can tell you this much: I've seen more changes in my time than I care to remember, and not all were for the best, but there are changes afoot in this house that *are* good."

George didn't have a clue what she was talking about. "What changes, Grandma? What's good about them?"

She tapped her nose as if she were the keeper of some great mystery. "Mark my words, boy."

If she'd guessed George was talking about the Goffins moving out, she didn't seem very upset. But then, she wouldn't miss them like he would. All she did was leave food out for them in the fancy basket on the bird table. Or maybe she really did just leave it for the birds and had no idea that Lofty hooked it up from the roof with his fishing line.

Grandma Peggy felt in her bedside cupboard for her purse. "Can you go to the shops for me, please?" she asked. "I need two more balls of this wool, a newspaper, some matches ... oh and some sweets for yourself, for going."

She pressed a twenty pound note into his hand.

"Buy Baby Lofthausen a little gift with the change," she said. "What is it?"

"It's a G...irl." said George. He'd almost said 'Goffin'.

"You don't sound too sure," said Grandma.

"Oh, I'm sure," said George. "She's called Valley. Short for Valerie, I think."

It wasn't though. It was a proper Goffin name. Like all Goffins, Valley was named after a part of the place that kept them safe and secret: the roof over their heads. Oh, ... he was going to miss them all so much.

"Off you go, boy," said Grandma. "Don't sit there dwelling on things – it makes you look gormless. Get on with it!"

George stuck the twenty pound note in his pocket and whistled to Rex.

CHAPTER THREE

FLOODS AND FIZZY SHARKS

George set off on his bike with Rex running along behind him. It was bitterly cold and by the time he got to the shops his knuckles were blue. He parked his BMX, blew on his frozen fingers and went into Mr Shah's grocery shop.

"No dogs allowed, please," said Mr Shah. "Don't want him licking my loaves."

"It's alright. Rex doesn't like bread," explained George.

"Health and safety," insisted Mr Shah. "Kindly pick him up at least."

George bundled Rex into his arms. When

he'd had Rex as a puppy, he could hold him in one hand, but now he'd grown so much George wasn't sure how he was going to carry him as well as the shopping.

"Do you sell wool, Mr Shah?" he asked as Rex tried to lick the freckles off his nose.

The shopkeeper waved to a shelf groaning with all sorts of items for sale, none of which were even remotely related. "Knitting wool is over there, next to the frying pans."

George loved shopping here. It was like going on an archaeological dig crossed with a treasure hunt. As well as the usual newspapers, sweets and stamps, Mr Shah stocked everything from saris to sink plungers and spud guns; there was no knowing what you might find.

The wool was indeed next to the pans, and sitting on the same shelf was a teddy bear in a cellophane box. It was cross-eyed and had clearly been there for a while because the lid was dusty. George looked at the price label and noticed that one had been stuck on top of another. The bottom label had come from a completely different era and was in old money: twelve shillings and sixpence. The top one said twelve pounds and sixty pence.

"How much for the bear?" called George.

43

Unlike the cashiers at the supermarket in town, Mr Shah was usually willing to do a deal. George did a quick sum in his head. Two balls of wool was a fiver. The local newspaper Grandma Peggy wanted only cost a few pence, and so did the matches, but if the teddy bear cost twelve pounds sixty he would be left with less than two quid for sweets. That wouldn't buy many jelly snakes for Lofty and Eave.

Trying not to drop Rex, George stuck the bear in the box under his chin, balanced the balls of wool on top and shuffled over to the counter.

"I'll give you a fiver for the teddy," he said, putting it on the counter. It would make a lovely gift for Valley.

"No, no, no," said Mr Shah. "You're joking me. Ten pounds!"

When George lived in London, he often used to hang out at the street market with his mates. His friend Warren never paid full price for anything – he always haggled. George had never dared to do it himself because the market traders were quite scary. Mr Shah, on the other hand, was very smiley, so George decided to use the techniques he'd learned from Warren and meet him halfway.

"This bear is cross-eyed," George said. "I'll give you eight pounds and not a penny more."

"Nine pounds," said Mr Shah. "It has a most unique expression. They don't make them like that any more."

George dug his heels in. "Eight-fifty."

"For real mohair? You are robbing me blind," said Mr Shah.

He took out a duster and flicked the top of the box with it.

"It's a gift for the homeless," said George. He felt a bit bad saying it, but it seemed to do the trick. Mr Shah muttered something in Gujarati and put the teddy in a carrier bag with the wool. George wandered over to the pick-'n'-mix stand. Unfortunately Rex was wriggling so much while George was scooping the fizzy sharks into a paper cup he dropped several on the floor along with a scattering of rainbow drops. Mr Shah flew round the counter before George could upset the candy shrimps.

"You hold the dog, I'll hold the scoop. What is it you want, young man?"

"Thanks," said George. "I'll have two jelly snakes, two Dip Dabs, two liquorice pipes, some strawberry lips, a sweet necklace,

a load of those flying saucer things with the sherbet in and some Black Jacks, please."

He was going to give them to Lofty and Eave for Christmas. George was just wondering whether or not he'd have time to make them each a stocking to hang at the end of their beds when he remembered the rest of Grandma's shopping.

"And this newspaper and some matches, please," he said as Mr Shah weighed the sweets. "That'll be nineteen pounds and fifty pence exactly. Rotten news about Duke's Farm, isn't it?" he said, tapping the paper. "Who will supply my free-range eggs now that the floods have forced him to move out?"

"Farmer Duke has gone?" said George, somewhat surprised.

When George discovered that Rex came from a litter at Duke's Farm, he had ridden up there and offered all his pocket money to keep the puppy. Farmer Duke wouldn't take a penny though, and George had always been grateful to him for that.

He scanned the front page of the paper. It seemed that the recent heavy rains had caused severe flooding and the water had ruined the ground floor of the farmhouse. Farmer Duke, who was nearly eighty, had decided enough was enough and retired to Spain.

"I wonder if he took his dog?" said George out loud. "She was my dog's mum."

Mr Shah rolled the paper up and dropped it into the bag with a box of matches. "All I know is that no one in their right mind will buy that farm now. If it floods again they will lose everything."

"An abandoned building..." mused George.

"In a conservation area," added Mr Shah.

"So nobody can even knock it down or build on the land."

"Really?" said George. "That's brilliant! Thank you, thank you!" Mr Shah seemed rather perplexed by his reaction but it was the best news George had had all day: here was the answer to his prayers.

"Come on, Rex!" he cried, running out of the shop despite being weighed down by several kilograms of dog and shopping. With the carrier bag dangling over his handlebars and Rex bounding along behind, he pedalled off in the direction of Duke's Farm.

Bubbies and Baubles

It only took ten minutes
to cycle there but it was
quite hilly and he was
so excited that by the
time he arrived he was
all puffed out. Only this
morning he'd been in
despair, certain that
Lofty and Eave would
have to move far away
to find a suitably large,

derelict building for their extended family
to live in. Just a few hours later, here he was,
looking at the perfect location. Duke's Farm
wasn't as close as his attic, but it was only a
short bike ride away. He could probably walk
there in half an hour.

George got off his bike and leant it against
the old farm gate. The barnyard was eerily
silent. The only figure he could see was an
old scarecrow in the kitchen garden, which
had lost its jacket and hat. The last time

George had been here, there were chickens, goats and a dog. Now there were no animals to be seen apart from a donkey in a distant field, which belonged to the riding school.

As he approached the farmhouse, George noticed a tidemark level with the windowsills on the ground floor, where the flood waters had risen and subsided. Ice had formed on the remaining puddles; George shivered and put his hood up. He hoped it wouldn't be too damp for the Goffins if they moved in here with a baby.

51

Bubbies and Baubles

He huffed on a dirty
window, rubbed it with his
sleeve and peered inside.
He saw an old armchair
and a table paddling
in a few centimetres of
dirty water. A wooden
pipe floated on the surface along
with a dog bowl and some lumps of coal that
had washed out of the fireplace.

The paperbacks on the bottom shelf of
the bookcase were coated in dark slime and
George could see a solitary bright square
of paint against the yellowing wall where
a picture had hung for many years. Farmer
Duke must have rescued it and taken it with
him to Spain.

George wondered if it had been a portrait
of a relative, like the one Eave had found
in Grandma Peggy's attic, featuring his
Great-Great-Grandpa Montague fighting
a polar bear. Maybe the missing painting

was of Great-Great-Grandpa Duke. The
farm had been run by the same family for
generations – goodness knows what was
stashed away in this loft.

George gave the front door a push. The
latch wasn't on but he had trouble opening
it because the wood had swollen with the
damp. He gave it a hard shove then picked his
way across the front room, trying not to get
the inside of his trainers wet. When he
stepped on the bottom stair, foul
water squished up around
his foot, but beyond that the
staircase was dry.

"This can all be sorted,
Rex," he said, as the dog
followed him upstairs,
sniffing at the interesting
collection of smells
that had accumulated
in the carpet over
the century.

George leaned over the banister to get an aerial view of the front room – it needed an awful lot of cleaning, but he would do it. He didn't want Lofty and Eave to have any excuse to turn the place down. If he mopped up the water, ripped up the smelly carpet and found some dry logs in one of the barns to light a fire, the farmhouse would soon dry out.

But it was the state of the loft that was the most important thing. Even if the nearest inhabited cottage was several fields away, no Goffin would ever risk living Down Below for fear of being caught. Having no idea what a mess it might be in or even if the roof was still intact, George crossed his fingers and made his way up the second flight of stairs to the top of the house.

To his delight, there was an attic bedroom built into the eaves, rather like his own at Grandma Peggy's, but twice the size. Instead of there being a small green door that led

to the loft, there was a large green one
and, oddly, the paint smelled fresh. George
dabbed it with his finger: it felt slightly tacky
and, when he looked closely, he saw it had
captured his fingerprint.

He told himself the paint had just been
softened by the general dampness in the air,
and was just about to enter the loft when Rex
pricked up his ears and started scratching at
the door. George couldn't hear anything.

"Mind out, Rex," he tutted, turning the
handle. "It's only rats."

But it wasn't.

CHAPTER FOUR

DONKEYS
AND DARING

The attic was in darkness, but there was a
familiar smoky smell as if someone had just
snuffed out some candles. George felt in his
carrier bag for the box of matches and lit one.
The short glimpse he got of the loft in the
match flare made him gasp.

It was huge and, if he hadn't known better,
George would have thought there was just
a load of junk that had been sitting there
for years, but the bric-a-brac was in some
kind of order. It was as if someone had been
interrupted in the middle of arranging it into
separate rooms...

Bubbies and Baubles

Trash and hide? he wondered.

The match burnt George's thumb and he dropped it. He was about to reach for another one when he saw something glowing in the gloom. It was coming towards him.

"Who ... who's there?" he stammered.

"Halloo, Jowge ... 'tis yourself, yay?"

It was Arch, only he wasn't wearing his cassock this time. He was dressed in a pair of Farmer Duke's green wool trousers and a battered jacket and hat that had once belonged to the scarecrow. He lifted up the oil lamp he was carrying to George's face. Satisfied that it was really him, he grinned broadly and hung the lantern on a brass hook shaped like a horse head.

"I can't believe you're here!" exclaimed

George. "How did you even know this place was empty? It's nowhere near the belfry."

"Goodly news be travellin' swift," said Arch, making a big fuss of Rex. "There be Goffins livin' aloft in yonder barn – the Thatchers," he said casually, pointing into the distance. "Themselves be tellin' us that Himself Below be leavin' this dwellin'."

"The Thatchers? Oh yeah, your dad mentioned them," remembered George. "They were the ones who told us Rex had come from here. They sent Eave a message with Chimbley."

"Lo! Howfor be myne first-ever sister?" asked Arch. He climbed a ladder and took Farmer Duke's old pipe lighter out of his pocket to light a ring of candles that he'd nailed to a cart wheel and hung on a chain from the rafters.

"Eave's fine," said George, gazing at the curious antique farming implements in the candlelight. "How's your ... second-ever sister?"

"Valley be a fine bubby!" said Arch proudly, shinning down the ladder. "Smincey as a meece but most feisty!"

"Is her hair copper like Eave's?" asked George.

"Nay, 'tis goldin," said Arch. "Goldin as a buttycup."

George felt another wave of jealousy. Part of him felt it was soppy for a boy to go all gooey over a baby but Arch seemed perfectly happy to share his feelings.

"Myne heart be near to burstin' when Valley be borned, Jowge," he said, picking up a chair he'd turned over in a fit of panic when he'd heard Rex at the door earlier. "Herself be the most beautifill bubby myneself did ever see."

George couldn't hold back any longer. "You're so lucky!" he blurted. "You've got two sisters now. I haven't even got one!"

He turned his back and wandered off through a maze of butter churns, bridles and apple boxes. It wasn't just that he was jealous of the baby – as much as he liked Arch, he felt really annoyed that he'd got to the massive, magnificent attic at Duke's Farm before him.

George had wanted to be the one to find the Goffins a new home so they'd always remember him as their hero. It was the least, the last, the most important Kindness he could ever do for them and now it looked like Arch was about to take the glory away from him.

61

"Jowge," said Arch, struggling to shift an old brass bed. "Myneself can't be doin' this alone."

"Thought you were ox-strong," said George sarcastically. "That's what Eave says."

There was a slight pause.

"'Tis nothin' to what herself be callin' you, Jowge."

Did George detect a hint of envy in Arch's voice? He couldn't imagine for one second why anyone would be jealous of him.

"Jowgie this, Jowgie that," continued Arch, dragging the bed along by its posts and mimicking his sister. "Jowge be spear-sharp, Jowge be saintlee, Jowge be myne hero."

"Did Eave really say
that?" George was
taken aback. "When?"
He grabbed the posts
at the other end of
the bed. It was much
easier to lift with two
of them.

"Herself be forever scribblin'
to us about your wonderfill self," said
Arch. "Yourself be a normous hard act to
follow, Jowge."

"What, *me?* No, I'm not. You know what
they used to call me at my old school in
London? Weedy Carruthers!"

Suddenly, Arch scowled and dropped his
end of the bed. His gooseberry-green eyes
flashed and he put his fists up and danced
about like a boxer.

"Fi! Howfor *darst* themselves be mockin'
myne oh-nee step-in brother!" he raged.
"Myneself will be punchin' out their lights!"

"Steady," said George. "I thought Goffins were peace-loving people."

"Peacefill? Yay, 'til us be riled!" growled Arch. "Nobiddy darst cuss myne fambily. Yourself is myne fambily, yay, Jowge?"

George was so honoured that Arch considered him to be part of his family, he found himself nodding in agreement. No one had ever leapt to his defence like that before, so in the spirit of brotherhood he put his jealousy aside.

"Right, let's get this loft sorted, Arch. How many bedrooms do we need to arrange?"

George reckoned five: one each for Eave, Arch and Granny Cloister, a big one for Lofty and Ariel, and a nursery for Valley.

"Myneself be thinkin' six," suggested Arch. "For when yourself be stayin' over."

George made a window out of his fingers

and cast his eyes over the loft space. "There's enough room, isn't there? We could make bed bases out of those wooden pallets and mattresses out of the straw in the barns."

"Yay, and us could be usin' that normous beer barril for catchin' roof-rain indoors – myneself must be runnin' a pipe from the gutter..."

Their ideas were flowing but it was going to take an awfully long time to get the place ready to live in. Arch had already started on the kitchen, but there was still a bathroom, a separate toilet of some sort and a sitting room to make.

"How long do you reckon till it's finished?" asked George.

Arch sucked in his cheeks and closed one eye to aid his concentration. "Springtimes. Earlier if yourself be doin' some labourin'."

George agreed to do what he could. "I'm back at school after Christmas but I'll be able to help at weekends."

Bubbles and Baubles

Spring was a long time to wait. By then, Valley would be three months old. Lofty and Eave would never have seen her when she was new. It seemed such a shame. The more George thought about it, the more he could feel one of his grand plans coming on.

His parents and Grandma Peggy were supposed to be visiting friends in town for dinner on Christmas Eve. He'd been invited too and was dreading it. But what if he told them he was going carol singing with Hans Lofthausen instead? It was a brilliant excuse. When everyone had left the house, he could bring Lofty and Eave down from the loft and they could walk to Duke's Farm together.

"Arch?" said George. "If you could get your Uncle Garret to look after Granny Cloister for the evening, is there any way you could bring Ariel and the baby down here tomorrow as soon as it gets dark?"

Arch looked up from the
tin of nails he was sorting
through.

"Tomorrow? Whyfor
so soon?"

"Eave's desperate
to see Valley. It
would be her best
Christmas present
ever."

The Goffins didn't
really celebrate
Christmas in the
religious sense, but Yuletide
was an important part of their calendar
when they gave thanks for the harvest,
whether it be grown in the roof garden,
fished from the roof or found in the loft.

"'Tis a long way for Muppy to be walkin'
so soon after birthin'," said Arch. "Alack,
myneself doesn't have time to be buildin'
a cart."

"Is there nothing with wheels in one of the barns?" asked George.

"Oh-nee an olde tractor," said Arch. "But myneself cannot be reachin' the pedils."

Both boys sat down and racked their brains. There had to be a way.

"Myneself has it!" announced Arch, leaping out of his seat. "Myne muppy will be ridin' on yonder heehaw."

"Heehaw?" said George. "What ... you mean the donkey?"

"Yay! Myneself has a horse sittle," said Arch, pointing to an old saddle lying among a load of dusty horse tack.

"Darst say there be some rope somewhere..."

"You're going to *lasso* the donkey and ride it to the belfry?" laughed George in disbelief. "What if you get caught?"

"Myneself does live in dread of being cotched," admitted Arch. "But if us darst not be darin', us might as well be deaded, nay?"

It was agreed then: Arch would stay at the farmhouse that night and the next morning to make the place as welcoming as possible, then he'd fetch his mother and baby sister on the donkey while George brought Lofty and Eave on foot.

"Come, Jowge," said Arch, handing him a mop and bucket. "Whilst yourself be a-moppin' down below, myneself be-fetchin' some applewood. 'Twill be makin' a most sweet-smellin' fire."

"What if someone sees the smoke?" worried George.

Arch wrinkled his nose and laughed. "Scarecrows can't be speakin' and heehaws won't be tellin'! As for yonder cottage, 'tis empty. Themselves be long-gone, visitin' rellies for Yuletide."

George went downstairs and got to work. He mopped, wrung, cleaned and scrubbed until his hands were raw and his jeans were worn through from kneeling. He was trying so hard to get everything done, he hadn't noticed what time it was.

"Yourself best be goin' now, yay?" said Arch. "Afore your fambily be missin' you."

As George rode off on his bike with his shopping on the handlebars and Rex at his heels, he felt so happy he barely noticed the cold.

He couldn't wait to tell Lofty and Eave the great news. It was only when he got home that he realized quite how late it was.

"George! Where on earth have you been?" asked his mum. "I was worried sick."

CHAPTER FIVE

CAROLS AND CARDIGANS

"Sorry I'm late. I've been to see Hans," said George, thinking quickly. "He's got a new baby sister."

His mother's face softened. "Oh, how lovely! What's her name?"

"Val...erie. Valerie Lofthausen," said George, showing her the contents of his carrier bag. "I bought her this teddy on the way back. I'll give it to her tomorrow night. Hans wants me to go carol singing."

He thought he'd better mention it as soon as possible or his mum would insist on dragging him off to the Morrisons' on

Christmas Eve. She looked at him sideways.

"*Carol* singing? You've never been carol singing in your life."

"It's for a very good cause. It's for the homeless. Hans goes every year and I said I'd go with him because he's moving back to Berlin in the spring.

"I'll ring Mrs Morrison and tell her you're not coming then," said his mum. "Good for you, George. I can't imagine what it must be like to be homeless in this weather – what happened to your trousers?"

George looked at the holes in his jeans where he'd been kneeling to scrub Farmer Duke's cobbles. "Fell off my bike," he said. "It's icy... Get off me, Mum, I'm fine!"

When his mother had finished examining him for cuts and bruises,

he took the shopping to Grandma's room.
She looked a bit cross.

"What time do you call this, boy? Not much
point reading that paper you got me now –
it'll be yesterday's news. Did you
get my wool?"

George put it on the
bedside table next to
her needles.

"What are you
knitting, Grandma?"
It looked like a tiny
cardigan.

"Oh, just a little
something," she said.

George smiled to himself. Grandma Peggy
couldn't fool him. When he'd mentioned that
his friend had a new baby sister, she must
have guessed the friend was Eave, which
meant that she *did* know about the Goffins.
Why else would she be knitting baby clothes?

"Is it a cardigan for Hans's baby sister?"

Either Grandma Peggy didn't hear him
or she deliberately changed the subject.

"Did you get my matches?"

George had left them at Duke's Farm,
in the attic.

"Sorry, forgot. I bought you
some fizzy sharks, though."

He fished a couple of jelly
shapes out of the pick-'n'-mix
tub by way of an apology.

"Fizzy sharks?" muttered Grandma.
"Did I get any change?"

George gave her a fifty pence coin.

"There would have been more, but I bought
this teddy," he explained. "It was a real
bargain. The fur's mohair."

"It's got gozzy eyes," she said. "Never mind.
Who's it for? Don't tell me, Hans Lofthausen's
baby sister?"

Grandma raised her eyebrows and gave
George one of those looks that meant she
could see straight through him.

"Give her my love," she said, averting her eyes to the paper. "It says here, Farmer Duke has gone to Spain and left his farm to rot. Well, I never."

George took the teddy bear up to the attic to tell Lofty and Eave the brilliant news. They were almost overcome with excitement to hear he'd found the perfect new home for their whole family. When he mentioned that Arch was already there, sorting everything out so they could move in  the following spring, Eave jumped up and down on the chaise longue so hard that one of the legs broke.

"Becalm yourself, myne Littley!" Lofty scolded gently. "Afore yourself be trashin' the place. Us might not be be needin' it much longer, but somebiddy might."

Eave handed him the broken chair leg and lowered her head apologetically.

"Sorree Pappy, only myneself be sooo gleefill!" Unable to contain her excitement, she started dancing up and down on the spot. "Be there a bed at Duke's Farm for myneself, Jowgie?"

"There's room for six bedrooms," George told her. "The loft is enormous."

Lofty took off his busby and shook his head in amazement. "*Six* chambers? What riches! 'Tis a palace, nay?"

"Us will be livin' like kings and quoons!" squealed Eave, dancing around with the teddy bear. As she was still wearing her fur coat, she looked like she could be its mother.

Just when Lofty and Eave thought things couldn't possibly get any better,

George delivered the rest of his news.

"There's more," he said. "Tomorrow night, I'm taking you both to see the baby. It's all arranged."

He knew they'd be pleased, but he wasn't entirely prepared for their reaction. Eave stopped dancing and the two of them stared at him with their mouths open. They must have stopped breathing while George explained the plan to them because suddenly they both closed their eyes and fell backwards onto the bearskin rug by the mantelpiece. George panicked. For one terrible moment he thought they'd died of shock, but after a few seconds they came round, looking rather groggy.

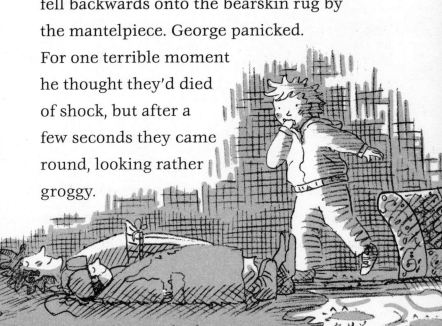

Bubbies and Baubles

"Ooh ... wherefor be myneself?" mumbled Eave.

"You're in Grandma Peggy's attic," said George. "You fainted."

Lofty sat up.

"Goodly morn, Jowge. Myneself must have fallen a-snooze. 'Twas a most wonderfill dream," he yawned. "Myneself be dreamin' us be goin' to see Valley and Ariel."

"We are!" laughed George. "It's not a dream." He finally got Lofty and Eave to believe him and, before he left to go to bed, promised to collect them the following evening as soon as it was safe to leave.

* * *

The next morning was Christmas Eve, and George was woken by the banging of the bathroom door. It sounded as if his mother still had a tummy bug. His heart sank. If she wasn't well enough to go to the Morrisons' he wouldn't be able to get the Goffins out of the house.

George found her in the kitchen. She was eating dry toast in her dressing gown.

"Are you alright, Mum?" he asked. "Are you going to be well enough to go to the Morrisons'?"

"I'm fine," she said. "Why? Have you changed your mind about carol singing? Why not come to the Morrisons' with us? There will be plenty of food."

"I would do," said George. "But I can't let down Hans and the homeless, can I?"

His mother gave him a half-smile as if she suspected he'd never wanted to go in the first place, and for a few moments George was certain she didn't believe him about the carol singing.

"Mum, it will be Hans's last Christmas here."

She dug out a thermos flask. "Alright, I'll warm up a tin of soup for you later," she said. "You can take that and some mince pies. Oh, and give this Yule log to Mrs Lofthausen – does she like chocolate?"

"She likes crisps," said George, opening the food cupboard to see what was in there that the Goffins might enjoy. "And she's very fond of shortbread and – what are these?"

"Florentines."

"They're Mr Lofthausen's favourite," said George. "When will you be back tonight?"

"The Morrisons are insisting we go to midnight mass," she groaned. "Don't forget to hang your stocking up, George."

"Aren't I a bit old for all that?" he said.

His mother put her head on one side. "No one's too old. What do you want for Christmas?"

"A baby sister," he said without hesitating. "Or a brother. I don't mind which."

She smiled and ruffled his hair. "Really? And there was me thinking you wanted a PlayStation Three."

When she left, George finished raiding the cupboards, then went back to his room and spent the rest of the morning doing festive things. He made a card for Grandma, then a paper chain, which he draped around his computer. He found a pair of old football socks, decorated the tops with cotton wool to make them look like snowy Christmas stockings and filled them with pick-'n'-mix for Lofty and Eave.

Then, after a late lunch, he went to see them in the attic. Lofty was in the middle of carving something – a gift for Arch, he said – and Eave was packing baby items into a case. While they were busy, George made an excuse to secretly go and hang the stockings on the end of their beds.

"Can I use your loo, Eave?"

"Us closet? Yay, yourself be knowin' where 'tis, Jowge."

When he came back, Eave was sitting at an angle on the now three legged chaise longue looking at an old photograph album.

The photos were sepia and as she turned the tissue paper between the pages, George realized they were all of the same baby girl.

"Whose baby is that?" he asked.

Eave traced the little chubby face with her finger. "Herself did belong to your Great-Great-Grandplods."

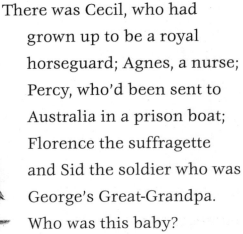

Eave had worked out George's family tree from the paperwork and pictures she'd found in the loft, so George knew his Great-Great-Grandma Maud had given birth to six children.

There was Cecil, who had grown up to be a royal horseguard; Agnes, a nurse; Percy, who'd been sent to Australia in a prison boat; Florence the suffragette and Sid the soldier who was George's Great-Grandpa. Who was this baby?

"'Tis Victoria Madeleine Carruthers," said Eave, quietly.

"Cute," said George. "What did she grow up to be?"

Eave lowered her head. "Herself never did grow up, Jowge. 'Twas scarlit fever carried her off. Myneself did find a mournin' card and certifikit."

George felt his eyes prickle. A baby had died in his family and he'd only just found out. He didn't know her and it was long, long ago but even so, she was a relative. There was a connection; how could he not feel sad? Eave kissed the picture of the infant.

"Poor little kid," said George.

There he'd been, hating Christmas and moaning about losing his childhood, when baby Victoria hadn't had either. He understood that people died of old age – like his Grandpa Gordon – but why this little baby? His mum was a nurse; she often worked in the baby clinic, giving babies vaccinations so they wouldn't get sick. He touched the mark on his arm where he'd had his own jabs against measles, mumps and rubella. If only Victoria had been vaccinated, maybe she'd have lived to see lots of Christmases.

Eave squeezed his hand. "'Tis most sorrowfill, Jowgie, but bubbies often be dyin' of vile lurgies in yestertimes. Themselves be lackin' in goodly cures."

"Yay," added Lofty, stepping out from behind the book case, "but happilee, bubbies be havin' besterly medicine nowatimes and mostlee be livin' to a ripe old age."

Grandma Peggy was always telling George about the good old days, but she rarely mentioned the bad bits, like babies dying.

"Times be most hard for littleys in ye olden days," said Eave. "Has yourself never be readin' *Twisted Olives* by Charlie Dicken?" she waved an old book at him.

"You mean *Oliver Twist*?" said George.

"I saw the musical." George wasn't a great one for reading and, anyway, Charles Dickens' stories about poor children living in the workhouse were just make-believe, weren't they?

"Nay, Jowge, Charlie Dicken be most truthfill!" exclaimed Eave, opening the book and showing him an illustration of a thin little boy dressed in rags, trudging through the snow. "When your Great-Grandplods be alive, many littleys be starvin' and some be stuffed most crewilly up the chimbley..."

George felt a pang of guilt. How dare he feel sorry for himself? His parents had never once shoved him up a chimney, and he wasn't homeless, hungry or sick. He'd had a great childhood – he was still having it! He picked up the album again and looked at the baby's photo.

"I don't want her to be forgotten," he said.

"Herself never will be," said Lofty. "Myne Valley be needin' a goodly middil name.

Would yourself be doin' the honour of choosin' it, Jowge?"

"Victoria," he said, tracing the smiling face of the tiny girl with his finger. "Please will you call her Valley Victoria? Then whenever you say her name, I'll remember my baby Victoria."

"So will us all, Jowge," nodded Lofty approvingly.

"Forevertimes," promised Eave.

George closed the album and hugged it to his chest.

CHAPTER SIX

SNOW AND SOUP

Having turned down a lift to the
Lofthausens', George waved off his parents
and Grandma Peggy, promising to lock up
the house when he left to go carol singing.
As soon as the car had driven away, he ran
upstairs and knocked on the attic door.

Pom ... tiddy pom pom ... pom pom!

"Grab your lanterns, let's go!" he said,
swapping Lofty's enormous busby for one
of his old bobble hats and taking a bag
full of baby clothes from Eave.

Even though George had reassured them
that Grandma Peggy's house was empty

and would be for several hours, they were still nervous about leaving the loft and kept hovering on the stairs.

"Come on, the sooner we get there, the longer you can stay," said George, trying to chivvy them up. "We have to be back here by midnight."

Lofty growled at him through several layers of scarf. "Less haste! A Goffin Down Below be as cautious as a canary on a carpet."

"Ourselves isn't stair-savvy!" pouted Eave, clinging to the banister.

George realized he had no right to be impatient with them – they'd always been very understanding about his fear of heights on the occasions they'd invited him out onto the roof.

"OK, take your time," he said. "I'll fetch the soup. See you in the hall."

He nipped into the kitchen, grabbed the thermos and shoved it in his rucksack along with the teddy bear, his torch and the feast

he'd raided from the cupboard. Rex was
dozing in his basket but George thought he'd
like another trip to see the farm where he
was born, so he woke him up.

"Walkies, Rex!"

When he went
back into the hall,
he found Eave and
Lofty mesmerized by
the artificial snow
sprayed on the inside
of the front door.

"Jowge, howfor be
it snowin' indoors?"
asked Eave.

"It's not real," laughed George,
ushering them both out of the front door.
Normally, he'd have taken them round the
back, but it was dark and even if they were
seen by passers-by, what did it matter? People
would simply assume they were carol singers.
Lofty sniffed the air.

Bubbies and Baubles

"Us be havin' real snow afore midnight," he said. "Myne snitch be a-whiffin' it."

Walking as briskly as he could with Rex stopping to pee on every lamp post, George led the way up the lane and past the bridge. Lofty and Eave were quite slow walkers as it wasn't something they usually did much of, so it was almost seven o'clock by the time they reached the shops. They were all shut for Christmas now, apart from Mr Shah's. Eave stopped and pressed her nose to the window.

"Look, Pappy! Itself be havin' more treasure than Grandmuppy Peg's loft!"

"That's where I got the teddy bear from," said George.

There were loads of old teddies in the loft but George knew that all of her life, Valley would have second hand things. Just this once, he wanted her to have something new. He linked arms with Eave, partly because he was in a good mood and partly to drag her away from the shop window.

"If we walk really fast, we should be at the farm in about fifteen minutes," he said.

They took a short cut across the green where there were no street lamps, so they stopped and lit their lanterns. As they made their way through the trees a few snowflakes began to fall.

"Do you think we'll have a white Christmas, Lofty?" asked George. Lofty stood at the bottom of the hill and gazed up at the sky.

"Darst say. Here's hopin' itself won't be fallin' deep-drift for fear myne bubby be snowbound on a heehaw."

George's head had been so full of snowball fights, snowmen and the chance of a Christmas that looked like the ones in picture books, he hadn't thought about the danger.

"I bet it won't even settle," he said. "Anyone want some soup? It's tomato."

He poured some into the lid of the thermos and passed it around. Eave took a few sips and sat down. The bright red soup stain round her mouth made her face look even paler. George was a bit worried about her. Her main form of exercise was leaping about on the roof – she wasn't used to walking over rough ground.

"You OK, Eave?"

"'Tis nothin' to grumbil about. Myne legs be a bit weary," she said.

They still had to climb the hill. It wasn't that steep, but it probably seemed it to a Goffin. Putting the lid back on the soup, George gave his rucksack to Lofty.

"Stand on that stile, Eave. You can have a piggyback."

She looked at him in alarm. "Fi! Mynself will be ridin' a piggin?" She held her lantern up to see if she could see one in the nearby field.

"No, not a pig! It's just an expression," he said. "I'll carry you. Put your arms around my neck."

Bubbies and Baubles

She hardly weighed more than Rex and if she hadn't been wearing the heavy fur coat, he'd have probably made it up the hill without even breaking into a sweat. It was great fun running downhill though. Eave hung onto his ears, giggling.

"Faster, Jowgie, faster! Yourself be galompin' like a heehaw!"

Determined to prove that he was stronger and fitter than ox-strong, lark-swift Arch, George gathered speed, which would have been fine if he hadn't caught his heel on an icy puddle. As one of his feet flew up into the air he tried to catch his balance, but landed on his backside. The two of them eventually rolled to a stop in an undignified heap at the bottom of the hill.

Lofty, running to their rescue, skidded on the same patch of ice and landed on top of them. George sat up, rubbed his bruises and kicked his legs to make sure they were still working.

"Has anyone broken anything?"

Lofty was struggling to get up. "Yay. Myneself can't be movin', Jowge."

There was a pool of red oozing out from the back of his bobble hat.

"Lie still!' gasped George. "I think you've got a head injury. You're bleeding." With shaking hands, he searched in his pockets for a tissue and dabbed at the blood frantically, only to discover that it smelled of ... tomatoes!

"'Tis a terribil waste of soup," sighed Lofty as Rex licked his bobble hat. "Myneself be breakin' the thermoose."

Laughing hysterically,
George took the heavy rucksack off
Lofty and helped him up. Both the lanterns
had gone out, so he switched on his torch and
pointed the beam at Duke's Farm. Through
the swirling snow, they could see a faint wisp
of smoke curling out of the chimney.

"Themselves be here!" cried Eave.
"Muppy! Arch! Myne oh-nee sister!"

Forgetting how tired her legs were, she
grabbed George's hand and, holding onto
her hat, raced towards her new home and
knocked on the door.

"Whatever be keepin' yourselves?" grinned
Arch, welcoming them in. "Come, Muppy and
Valley be waitin' Up Above."

Bubbies and Baubles

George was amazed to see the transformation downstairs. The scent of applewood burning in the grate had removed the smell of damp, and the floorboards had almost dried out. The walls had been freshly whitewashed, a clean rug had been thrown down and fresh curtains had been hung.

"'Tis most wonderfill, Arch!" squealed Eave, clapping her hands together.

"Jowge be doin' the dirty work," said Arch, generously. "Wait till yourself be seein' the loft, Pappy, 'tis normous!"

Lofty was halfway up the stairs already, chuntering to himself. "Can't be waitin' a momint longer to be seein' myne Ariel and bubby."

Eave charged after him, trying to get in front, and George followed at what he hoped was a discreet distance. It was their baby after all – they should see her first.

"What's the code?" asked George as they reached the green door that lead to the loft.

Arch knocked.

Pom pom pom pompa - pom!

"'Tis open!" called Ariel, cheerily.

"In yourselves go," said Arch protectively. "Hush mind, lest Valley be a-dreamin'."

Eave and Lofty tiptoed in. George hesitated at the entrance, holding Rex's collar. Arch gave him a gentle shove.

"Go say halloo to your new step-in sister, yay?"

Ariel was sitting on an old rocking chair by
a little oil-burning stove in the half-finished
parlour. There in front of her, in a trough full
of hay, lay the tiniest baby George had ever
seen. The teddy he'd brought was bigger than
she was.

"Wow!" he said.

"Herself be most beautifill, yay?" said Eave,

touching Valley's golden curls as she slept. George nodded.

"Hello, Valley Victoria," he whispered.

She opened her eyes. They were blue, but there was already a hint of gooseberry-green. George held out his finger and she grasped it tightly in her miniature hand.

"Would yourself be likin' to cuddil bubby, Jowge?" asked Ariel. "Come sit whilst myneself be puttin' out the feast."

"Jowge be givin' us crispies, smincey pies, florences and logs!" said Eave, leaping up to help her mother.

"And shortbread," said George as he sat down on the rocking chair. He felt nervous. He'd never held a baby before. Cradling her head in one hand, Lofty put Valley gently in George's lap.

"Lo! Herself won't break, Jowge," he smiled, wandering off to explore the loft. "Myne fambily will be *most* joyfill here – six chambers? Such riches!"

* * *

The evening flew by. Pleasantly sleepy after
eating the Yuletide spread, swapping news
and playing party games, Lofty was just
having a quick snooze when there was an
almighty splintering noise. Part of the roof
had collapsed under the weight of snow.

"Fi!" wailed Ariel, ducking under the table
with the baby. "Us dwellin' be a-fallin'!"

"Nay, Muppy," said Arch. "Myneself be
guessin' 'tis oh-nee a rottin' timber."

He shinned up a
ladder to investigate.
There was an icy
draught coming
through the hole
but, despite the
disastrous turn
of events, Eave
couldn't help
giggling at Lofty
who was buried

in the avalanche up to his bobble hat.

"Pappy, yourself be lookin' like a snow genteelman!" she said, brushing him down.

"Yay, most hilarious," sulked Lofty, calling up to Arch. "Can yourself be fixin' it?"

"Not afore the snow be meltin', Pappy. Itself be fallin' most terribil heavy."

The Goffins couldn't stay overnight in a loft with no roof – not with a baby.

"What'll you do now, Arch?" sighed George. "Go back to the belfry on the donkey?"

Arch shook his head. "Nay! Himself be back in the stabil. Us can't be drivin' a heehaw in this, Jowge. Darst not risk it. If himself be trapped in a drift, Valley Victoria be catchin' poomonia!"

"Alack!" cried Eave. "Wherever shall us stay?" she looked across at George and suddenly her expression changed. "Aha! Myneself be havin' a grand idea ... Jowgie?"

"Ye–s," he said, guessing what she was going to ask him.

"Us could be squeezin' in at Grandmuppy Peg's, yay? 'Tis oh-nee for one night."

It had just crossed George's mind too. He couldn't think of a better solution and Grandma Peggy's was much nearer than the belfry – if they left now, even taking the snow into account, they could get back before his parents came home. But could Ariel walk that far?

"Myneself will be makin' a sleigh for Muppy and Valley to ride in," said Arch, holding up some piping, which he was already bending into runners. "Come, Jowge, be holdin' the torch while myneself be takin' the gate off."

"Myneself will be makin' skis," announced Lofty, searching through a pile of timber he'd found earlier.

"Hang on, though," said George, trying to be sensible. "What if you're in Grandma Peggy's loft and Valley starts crying? How am I supposed to explain *that* to Mum?"

"Yourself will be thinkin' of somethin', Jowge Carruthers," said Lofty. "Yourself always does."

But as George ran downstairs to help Arch make the sledge, he had serious doubts.

CHAPTER SEVEN

SATSUMAS AND SLEIGHS

George went outside and held the torch
while Arch unscrewed Farmer Duke's front
gate. It was amazing how much snow had
fallen in such a short time. The barnyard and
the fields beyond were already completely
whited-out; all the hedgerows blurred, all the
night sounds muffled by a thick winter coat.

Rex had never seen snow before. He
pounced on the drifts and tunnelled through
them with his nose, sneezing and snorting,
then went to see what the boys were doing.

"Oh, look at you!" laughed George, picking
the icicles out of Rex's fur.

Arch lay the gate on the ground, made some holes in the bent piping with a hammer and a nail then reached in his pocket for some screws.

"Pass myneself the screwin' driver, Jowge."

They attached the pipe runners to the gate sledge and flipped it over. All it needed now was something to pull it along by and a comfortable seat for Ariel to sit on. Arch ran indoors to fetch the saddle and bridle he'd put on the donkey earlier – they would be ideal.

"Ask Eave to come out," called George.

He doubted she'd ever had a chance to play in the snow, being a Goffin, so he quickly made a pile of snowballs and hid behind the old chicken coop. He only made soft ones – not like the rock-hard ammunition his friends used to

attack him with on the rare occasions it had snowed in London. She was a little girl; this would be a friendly fight.

He waited and waited in a crouched position until he got pins and needles in his leg. Eave must be too busy helping Ariel to be larking about with him. Just as he was about to stand up, something hit him on the back of the head with such force he almost fell over.

"Gotcha, Jowgie!" squealed Eave.

"Right, you've asked for it now!" he laughed.

He chased her across the farmyard, lobbing snowballs as fast as he could roll them but she zigzagged away like a rabbit and he missed his target everytime.

"Yourself will never be cotchin' me!" she teased, waggling her fingers by her ears. As soon as he gave up, she deliberately threw herself onto her back in the soft snow and waved her arms up and down.

"Myneself be a snow angil!" she grinned.

George fell on his back and copied her, pressing his shoulders into the snow to make wings. They lay together, gazing up at the stars with their mouths open, catching snowflakes on their tongues.

George bit his lip. "I'm going to miss you, Eave."

She didn't reply. She just reached out, held his hand and squeezed it. They stayed silent for a while, then she sat up and hugged her knees.

"Yourself will always be myne besterly friend, Jowge Carruthers," she said. "One day, when myneself be wed and has myne own bubby, us be movin' back into Grandma Peggy's forevertimes, yay?"

It was a lovely thought and George clung to it.

"I'll keep the roof garden going for you." He said, "And I'll never let my parents go in the loft," he said.

"Promise, Jowgie?"

"Yay. On my grandmother's life – and my mother's."

The talk of mothers made him spring to his feet.

"We'd better get a move on," he said. "There's a risk Mum might want to come home early if she's still feeling sick."

They brushed themselves down and by the time they'd run back to the house, the sledge was finished and Ariel was sitting proudly on it with Valley in her arms, wrapped in a cocoon of duvets and blankets.

"Ah, *there* yourselves be!" waved Lofty, balancing on a pair of wooden skis he'd knocked together. He was holding a smaller pair for Eave and a set of ski poles made from a couple of old umbrellas.

"Be slippin' into these, Littley!" he said. "Time be tickin' on."

Eave strapped the home-made skis onto her boots and, while Arch locked up, George helped Lofty pull the sledge towards the hill. It wasn't hard work for them – the wood probably weighed more than Ariel and Valley put together – but Eave was struggling to get up the slope on her skis.

"'Tis most steep!" she called. "Myneself be slippin' backaways, Pappy!"

George had a brainwave. Braving the chill as he lifted up his jacket and jumper, he took the belt off his jeans and attached it to Rex's collar.

"I'm sure he's got a bit of Husky in him!" he called. "Hold on to the belt, Eave – see if he'll pull you up."

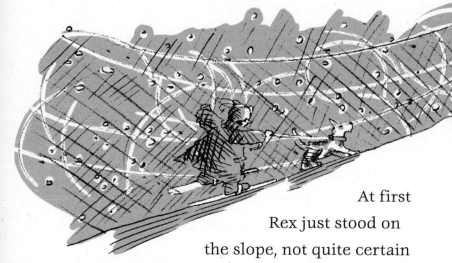

At first
Rex just stood on
the slope, not quite certain
what was being asked of him, but
with the aid of a leftover mince pie he soon
got the idea. George let him sniff the pastry,
then threw it up the hill as far as he could
and Rex bounded after it, with Eave in tow
trying desperately not to end up in the splits.

Happily, coming down the hill was a piece
of cake for the sledge and the skier, and after
that the terrain was relatively flat. With the
boys and Lofty taking it in turns to pull, they
were out of the woods, past the shops and
back at Grandma Peggy's house by eleven
o'clock.

Making sure the coast was clear, George hid the sledge and skis down the side of the house. He'd need the sledge to take Eave's mum and baby sister back the next night. Hopefully the snow would have stopped by then and Arch would have gone ahead early and fixed the hole in the roof at Duke's Farm. Ariel and Valley could stay there until the snow thawed enough to ride the donkey safely back to the belfry.

George unlocked Grandma Peggy's front door. Ariel was naturally nervous at being Down Below in a strange house.

"Come on, Ariel, it's lovely and warm," he said.

She stepped inside but, having never known the luxury of full central heating, she felt rather too warm. She adjusted her scarf and fanned herself.

"Ooh, 'tis like summertimes!" she said politely.

"Be showin' us your Yule tree, Jowge," begged Eave. "Does itself be a-lit with glowin' worms?"

"Nay, Littley, that be an olde Goffin tradition," added Lofty. "When myne ancient rellies be livin' on the Isle of Inishgoff, come Yuletide, themselves be cotchin' glowin' worms in papey lanterns. Themselves be lightin' the branches most brightlee."

"I don't think there are any glow worms in Grandma Peggy's garden," said George. "Only slugs."

"Darst say Jowge's tree be glowin' with candils," said Lofty. "Myneself be seein' 'em on ye olde Yule cards."

George shook his head. "No one puts candles on Christmas trees any more, Lofty. They're a fire hazard. Nowadays we use fairy lights."

Eave's eyes opened wide in amazement.
"Lo! Yourself be havin' *fairies*?"

"They're just little electric lights," he said.
"I'll show you."

What harm could it do, just this
once, to let them sit and look at the
Christmas tree for a few minutes while
his parents were out? He opened the
door, sat them down on the sofa in
the dark then crept behind the tree
and switched on the fairy lights.

A collective gasp of delight went
up from the Goffins. They
gazed at the tree in awe.

"'Tis most sparklin', Jowge!" sighed Ariel.

"See, Muppy? Itself be havin' an angil Up Above," said Eave. "Herself be real, nay?"

Even Arch was impressed. "Whofor be all those gifts under yonder branches, Jowge?"

George scuffled over on his knees and looked at the tags. "That big one's for me ... and that one ... and these. The rest are for Mum, Dad and Grandma Peggy." He held up a small round parcel, felt it and dropped it. It bounced up. "That one's for Rex."

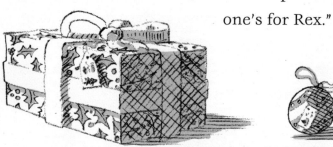

"Pappy?" whispered Eave. "Whyfor be Jowgie gettin' many gifts when myneself oh-nee be gettin' one? Has myneself been terribil bad?"

Lofty gave her a squeeze. "Nay, Littley.

Yourself be Pappy's angil but goodly Goffins be countin' blessin's, not boxes, yay?"

"That be the true meanin' of Yuletide," added Ariel.

Eave looked thoughtful, then she started counting on her fingers and mumbling to herself.

"Myne muppy ... myne pappy ... Grandmuppy ... Arch ... bubby Valley ... myne roof ... myne step-in brother..."

She put her hands on her hips and grinned.

"Yay! Myneself be havin' way more blessin's than yourself has boxes, Jowge," she boasted.

"The besterly gifts be havin' no wrappin's," nodded Lofty, bouncing Valley Victoria gently on his knee.

Bubbies and Baubles

A light, even brighter than a glow worm's, came on in George's head. Christmas wasn't about how many presents you got. He knew that now and, as he counted his own blessings, he felt blissfully Christmassy at last.

"Would anyone like a Brazil nut?" he beamed.

There were some assorted nuts arranged on a pretty dish on the coffee table. He handed it round and put the telly on. There was usually a good film showing on Christmas Eve. What he'd forgotten was that although Lofty and Eave had occasionally watched TV in his

bedroom, Ariel and Arch had never seen anything like it in their lives.

"There be peepil lookin' through its windypane," hissed Arch, leaping behind the sofa. Ariel buried her face in a cushion.

"Fi! Us will be cotched!" she wailed. "Trash and hide, Lofty, trash and hide!"

Eave, who reckoned she was far more sophisticated about these things than they were, casually cracked a hazelnut shell and explained.

"Don't be frettin' yourself! Themselves can't be seein' us. 'Tis oh-nee a fillum, yay?"

"Yay," said Lofty, putting his arm round his wife. "No cause for dread."

Bubbies and Baubles

Ariel sighed with
relief and put the
cushion back. Arch
pretended he'd
never been scared
at all and was
merely retrieving
a tree decoration that had

fallen behind the sofa. He twirled it in his
fingers and made it spin for the baby, who
fixed it with her huge eyes and gurgled.

"Valley be lovin' this bauble," he
said as the baby's tiny fingers tried
to grab it. It was an old, wooden one
with a snow scene painted on
it, suspended by a glittery silver
ribbon – George remembered
loving it when he was tiny too.

"She can keep it," he said. "Tell her I gave it
to her, then every Christmas when she hangs
it up at Duke's Farm, she'll see it and maybe
she'll remember me."

"Valley Victoria will never be forgettin' yourself, Jowge!" said Ariel. "Myneself and Lofty will be telling her how Jowge Carruthers braved wind an' snow so herself could be spendin' her first ever Yuletide with her fambily."

George felt himself swelling with pride, and it wasn't just all the nuts he'd eaten. Now the compliments were coming as thick and fast as the snow had earlier.

"Myneself will be tellin' Valley how Jowge be helpin' to make the sleigh!" added Arch, squeezing a satsuma segment so enthusiastically it squirted Lofty in the eye.

"And myneself will be tellin' Valley how Jowge be lookin' after her oh-nee big sister and pappy when they be livin' merrilee aloft at Grandmuppy Peg's!" declared Eave, eyeing up the chocolate shapes tied to the tree. George slipped one off a branch and gave it to her.

"Talking of Grandma Peggy," he started. "There's something I've been meaning to ask you for ages, Eave." Now was his chance. "Does Grandma know that you —"

Before he could finish the sentence, he saw the reflection of car headlights in the window. His parents were pulling up on the drive.

"Quick! Everybody run to the loft," panicked George, looking at the clock on the mantelpiece. "They're home early!"

Grabbing their bits and pieces and falling over each other in their hurry, Eave and Lofty shooed Ariel and Arch upstairs while George straightened the cushions and crawled round the carpet picking up the nutshells.

It always took a long time to get Grandma out of the car, what with her dodgy knees.

George was praying that by the time his dad
had got her walking frame out of the boot
and helped her through the snow, the Goffins
would have made it back up the three flights
of stairs and into the attic before his mum
could open the front door.

He hoped the snow had already filled
the Goffin footprints leading up the front
path – if not, he'd blame it on carol singers.
He mentally rehearsed what he'd been up to
during the evening with Hans Lofthausen
to try and get his story straight.

George thought he was just
about on top of everything
when his parents came
bowling in, with Grandma
Peggy following slowly
behind.

"Hi!" he said. "How come you didn't go to midnight mass?"

His father took his coat off and put some more coals in the fire grate. "Mr Morrison didn't want to risk getting his car stuck in the snow."

"Haven't seen snow like this since I was a nipper," Grandma said, manoeuvering herself into an armchair. "Did you make much money carol singing, boy?"

"Not a lot," said George.

"You've got a voice like a foghorn," she said. "You take after your father there. Your Grandpa Gordon, though, he had a beautiful singing voice."

George's mum rolled her eyes. "Never mind. It was all in a good cause," she said. "Can Hans sing, George?"

"Yes, he's a choir boy. I think I'll go to bed now," he said, excusing himself so he could sneak into the loft and spend the rest of the evening with the Goffins.

"Yes, off you go or Father Christmas won't come, will he?" smiled his mother. "What's that little thing doing on the floor?"

It was one of Valley's pink knitted bootees! She must have kicked it off while they were watching telly. His mum held it up and looked at it quizzically.

"Where on earth did that come from?"

George could feel his face going bright red. She was waiting for an answer.

CHAPTER EIGHT

BRUSSELS AND BOOTEES

George stared at the baby bootee his mum was holding and gulped.

"I expect he picked it up by accident at Hans's house," said Grandma, coming to his rescue. "Is it Baby Lofthausen's, boy?"

"Of course!" said George, smacking his forehead in mock disbelief that he could have forgotten such a thing. "It's Valerie's. I found it on the bathroom floor at Hans'. I was going to give it back to his mum but I shoved it in my pocket and forgot."

"Easily done," said Grandma. "And I suppose it was you who ate all the satsumas?"

"Sorry," said George. "And the nuts."

"Didn't leave any for the birds then," muttered Grandma Peggy.

George was sure she was playing with him, referring to the Goffins in a roundabout way, but he couldn't catch her eye.

"Have you only had tomato soup?" asked his Mum. "Didn't Mrs Lofthausen give you any dinner?"

"Yeah," said George. "We had roast lederhosen but it wasn't very nice."

His mother pulled a face. "Lederhosen? I thought they were leather shorts."

"Really? No wonder it was tough," said George airily, backing out of the lounge. "Night then. See you all in the morning."

He went upstairs to his room, grinning with relief – despite the fact that he knew very little German, he appeared to have gotten away with it. He hung up his stocking and wondered if it would be full in the morning.

Technically it was already Christmas, as it had gone midnight. Father Christmas should have been and gone by now if he existed. Maybe he was like the Lofthausens, who could be conjured up at will to the point where they seemed so real, other people believed in them too.

In other years, George had tried to keep his eyes open all night so that he could see if it really was Father Christmas who filled his stocking. He must have fallen asleep every year though because, while he was convinced he'd never slept a wink, the stocking was always bulging with presents on Christmas morning and he'd never caught the culprit. He went over to the little green door opposite his bed and knocked.

Bubbies and Baubles

Pom ... tiddy pom pom ...
pom pom!

Eave let George in,
waving the stocking full of
pick-'n'-mix sweets that
he'd secretly hung at the
end of her bed – the one
with the Mickey Mouse
headboard that used to
belong to his dad when he was a child.

"Himself did come!" she squealed, her
eyes shining with excitement. "Pappy Yule be
comin' down the chimbley and bringin' me a
jelly serpent and fizzy saucers and all sorts!"

"You must have been a very good girl,"
said George, entering the attic. "Did Lofty get
anything?" he asked, knowing full well that
he had.

Lofty appeared with a liquorice pipe stuck
in his mouth. To George's horror, he was
trying to light it with the matches that George
had bought for Grandma.

"Yay, himself came, but myneself be danged if itself will be cotchin' a-flame." He waved the match over the pipe bowl, sucked furiously and watched in dismay as it melted in a black sugary mess and plopped on his slippers.

"You're meant to eat it, not smoke it!" explained George. The attic filled with a burnt treacley smell and Ariel wafted the sky light for a few moments to clear the air.

"'Tis a most homelee loft, Jowge," she said, winding baby Valley over her shoulder. "'Tis a great comfit to be knowin' myne oh-nee husband and daughter be dwellin' in such a fine place."

Bubbies and Baubles

"I love it here," said George. "You can't really see in the dark but Eave's made a brilliant job of the roof garden."

Even in the depth of winter, she was still growing vegetables in all sorts of containers she'd found in the loft: potatoes in a coal scuttle, winter cabbage in an old drawer, onions in a paddling pool.

In the past Eave had had to rely on her squirrel, Roofus to fetch fruit stones for her to plant, or the wind to blow seeds into the mud on the slates, but since she'd met George, he'd been bringing her half-used packs of seeds and beans found in rusty tins in Grandpa Gordon's shed. They were well past their grow-by date but the seeds didn't care; they grew anyway.

"Myneself shall be pullin'
taytoos for us Yuletide feast in the morn,
Muppy!" said Eave, taking Valley and
climbing up the ladder to show her Chimbley.
The pigeon was sound asleep in a pie dish in
the rafters.

"Taytoos?" said Ariel. "Myneself hasn't been
tastin' them for many a year. 'Tis all fern and
fungus in our neck of the woodlands. Has
yourself any fat for roastin' 'em, Littley?"

"Us be havin' normous lumps of besterly
butter," said Eave. "Pappy often be roof-fishin'
for it Down Below. 'Tis left in a basket on the
bird table."

Ariel pottered off to the kitchen to see what other edible delights she could find.

"I'll sneak you up some turkey to go with the spuds later," said George. "And some stuffing, and you can have all my Brussels sprouts."

"Yay!" said Eave. "Arch? Jowge be-fetchin' us all his russel spouts."

"Spouts?" said Arch, rubbing his stomach in anticipation. "Such treats! Myneself never be havin' those afore."

George had never known anyone look forward to sprouts so much and hoped they wouldn't be too disappointed with them. He decided he'd bring them some Christmas cake to take the taste away afterwards, and some presents for Arch and Ariel. His mother would probably get some perfume she didn't like and his father was bound to get some aftershave he'd never miss. Failing that, something was bound to fall out of a cracker that the Goffins would adore – a miniature magnifying glass, a pair of nail clippers or a cellophane fish that told fortunes.

"I'm going to make this the best Christmas ever!" said George, triumphantly.

"Yourself already has," said Lofty, patting him heartily on the back. "And now 'tis time for all goodly Goffins to be a-bed," he yawned. "Or us won't be fit for us feast."

George was tired too. Eave put Valley in his arms so he could give her one last cuddle before bedtime. He held her close to his chest and rocked gently, breathing in her powdery, baby smell.

"Happy Christmas, my oh-nee baby step-in sister," he whispered. Valley snuggled against him, closed her eyes and all was peaceful. But as soon as he tried to hand her back to Ariel, she woke up and started crying.

Bubbies and Baubles

It was the first time she'd cried all day and she was getting louder and louder.

"Herself be wantin' Jowge," panicked Ariel, trying to comfort her but Valley just cried louder and louder and now George could hear his mum calling from the hall. He flew out of the attic, shut the door behind him and climbed under the bedclothes still wearing his shoes.

He could still hear Valley yelling with the duvet over his head and now his mother was coming up the stairs. He had to do something to disguise the baby cries, so he faced the wall and pretended he was crying.

He felt his mother sit down on the edge of his bed, so he turned up the volume, sobbing as if his heart would break.

"George, whatever's wrong?"

"N...ot sure."

He didn't emerge until he'd poked himself in the eye sufficiently to produce some convincing tears. His mother put an arm round him as he lay heaving. It was a really nice feeling. She hadn't done that for a long time and because he was enjoying it so much, he carried on howling long after Valley had gone quiet.

"Hey, you've just got the Christmas blues," said his mum. "I get it too, you know. I think it's to do with wishing I could be a little kid again, just for one day."

143

George sat up and dried his eyes. He wasn't sure if his tears were real or not now. "Sorry for blubbing," he said. "I'm supposed to be eleven."

"Well, Grandma Peggy's a whole lot older than you and she always has a little cry at Christmas. Most people do," she said.

"Do they?" George thought it was just him being childish and silly.

"Even Dad wells up when he hears carols," said his mum. "'Away in a Manger' gets him every time."

She plumped his pillow and tucked his duvet in.

"It doesn't matter how old you are, George," she said. "You'll always be my baby, even when the new one comes along."

For a moment, what she'd just said didn't sink in. He thought he must have misheard.

"What did you just say, Mum?"

"I'm going to have a baby," she smiled. "In June."

So that's why she was being sick in the morning. She wasn't ill, she was pregnant. That's why Grandma Peggy was busy knitting baby jackets. George was speechless. He didn't know whether to laugh or cry so just sat there blinking. His mum's face fell.

"Oh. I thought you'd be pleased."

"Pleased?" He shook his head, but only because he couldn't believe that his dream had come true. He was going to have a brother or a sister. Finally, he would have someone to play with. Someone to look after. Someone who would look up to him.

"Mum? Best present ever!" he whooped.

At last, he would have someone he could talk to about Lofty and Eave. He couldn't wait to tell the Goffins and as it turned out, he didn't have to. As soon as his mum went back downstairs, someone tapped on the inside of small green door opposite his bed.

"Pom ... tiddy pom pom ... pom pom!"

He leapt up and opened it. Eave was standing there in her nightie, holding out a lace handkerchief that once belonged to his Great-Great-Grandma Maud. She put her head on one side and dabbed his eyes with it.

"Whyfore be yourself sobbin' afore, Jowge? Did Pappy Yule be leavin' no gift?"

George gave her a huge smile.

"Father Christmas gave me just what I've always wanted!" He said, punching the air, "I'm going to have a baby!"

Eaves' gooseberry-green eyes grew wider and wider as she took in the wonderful news.

"Rillytruly, Jowgie?"

"Really truly, Eave!"

She did a little dance on the spot, flung her arms around him and buried her head in his T-shirt.

"Uff ... uff ... uff... 'Tis a Yuletide miracle!" she sobbed.

But they were tears of joy. Her oh-nee step-in brother's greatest wish had finally come true and no one Up Above or Down Below could have been happier for him than his besterly friends, the Goffins.

Goffin Dictionary

A

a-blowin' blow, as in wind
accibump accident
afrit scared
a-loney lonely
afore before
alack oh dear, alas
aloft above
amberlance ambulance
angil angel
appil apple

B

be-accidents by accident
be-fall drop off, fall off
be-fallen fallen off
be-fetch retrieve, go and fetch
be-fix fix an item to something
be-guise disguise
be-morn in the morning
be-nights tonight, at night

be-scribe write
be-snuff snuff out
be-thunk thought
be-wilbered bewildered
be-yondertimes later on
besterly very best
betterly better than
bicycool bicycle
bide wait
binockles binoculars
biskies biscuits
bittilee bitterly
betwixt between
blam to hit hard
blankin's blankets
blisful lovely
bloomin's knickers/underwear
boggyman bogeyman
bomb-fired blown up, as with a bomb

borned to be born
botticks bottom
bottils bottles
boudoir bedroom
brainhat helmet
breakfeast breakfast
broilin' boiling
bubby baby
bulltough strong
butteries batteries
buttycup buttercup
buttyfly butterfly

C

candils candles
carefree relaxed
certificit certificate
chamber room
charitee kindness
cheery cherry
chickeree chicory
chimbley chimney, also
name of Eave's pet pigeon
chimbley egg pigeon's egg
choclick chocolate
choon tune or song
chrizzled christened
clamber climb
clangerin' making a noise

closet toilet
clucky egg hen's egg
cockerill cockerel
coddle cuddle
cometh is coming, has come
comftible comfortable
complicockled complicated
cotch, cotched catch, caught
cottin cotton
crafts skills
creepin' crawlin's insects,
invertebrates
crewilly cruely
crockydile crocodile
crumpilled crumpled
cuddil cuddle

D

dandyloon dandelion
darst not dare not
deaded killed

Goffin Dictionary

deadilly dangerous
demolishin' man
demolition man
dentipeep dentist
dishin's dishes
dinnin's dinner
do-long year all year
dockyments documents
does do
doin's bodily waste
dread fear – also dreadfill
dressin' maker dressmaker
drownded drowned

E

ebidle edible
eekwill equal
endelong lengthways
evertimes forever

f

fambily family
fearfill scared
feathies feathers
fi! exclamation of fear, help!
fillum film
fluttermouse pipistrelle bat
foul horrid

foxsharp wily
frizzled fried
fruitibles fruit

G

galomping galloping
gargled strangled
genteelman gentleman
ghoost ghost
gleefill gleeful
gnits gnats
goblit fancy cup
Goff-cart go-cart
Goffin race of people from Inish Goff, now sunk in the Irish Sea
goggils glasses
goldin golden
goobies gooseberries
goodly great, marvellous
grandmuppy grandma

grandpappy grandfather
grandplods grandparents
greatfill grateful
grinnin' taking the mick
grisly horrible

H

halloo hello
hamsom handsome
hanglebars handlebars
hark listen
has have
hastilee quickly
hath it has
haul a fishing catch, as in a haul of bird bread
head ouch headache
healthee healthy
heartilee heartily
heehaw donkey
hellishcopter hellicopter
himself he

hippopottimouth hippopotamus
hither here, as in come hither
honnee honey
hook take, steal
horse sittle saddle
horse tack bridle etc
houndbubby puppy
hounds dogs
howfor? how can we therefore?
hundrid one hundred

I

iggerant ignorant

J

jerkilee in a jerky manner
Jowge George
joyfill joyful
judgemint judgement

Goffin Dictionary

K

knickybockers bloomers

L

langwidge language
larfin' make fun of
larkswift swift as a lark
laydee woman
lemmin'aid lemonade
lessins lessons
lionbrave fearless
littley child, kid
lo! behold
long-a-long very long
Lundiner born in London
lurgies disease

M

magifryin magnifying
mammuth mammoth
marbils marbles
meatypaste meat paste
meece mouse
meecehole mouse hole
merrilee happily
merrimakin' having fun
mischeef trouble
miseree misery
moffs moths

morn morning
most very
motor car
munnee money
muppy mum
myne mine, belonging to me
myneself me, I

N

nakey without clothing
nay no
neighblies neighbours
neighbourly from the neighbourhood
newspapey newspaper
niddle needle
nightlie nightie
nightly at night time
nobiddy nobody
normous enormous
nowatimes nowadays
nutriments nourishing food

O

oh-nee only, if only

olde old

olden-day diggers archaeologist

once-a-time once

owlwise intelligent

ox-strong very strong

oziz ounces

P

pappy dad

parlour lounge

parrit parrot

peacefill peaceful

peacefun peaceful and harmless

pedil pedal

peek to look, observe, study

peepil people

per-lum plum

piggy toe

pilloows pillows

plummet to fall

plumptious plump

plush soft

ponky smelly

poomonia pneumonia

'poon harpoon

pricklepig hedgehog

poppin' corns popcorn

Q

quoons queens

R

raidi-who radio

rare unusual, unlikely

rarin' urgent desire to do something now

redded embarrassed

rellies relatives

riled angry

rillytruly to tell the truth

Roamin Roman

roly-round tied

roof-fish to fish from the roof for food or items

roof legs to have no fear of heights

rumpus noise

Goffin Dictionary

S

saintlee saintly
sammidge sandwich
sandils sandals
sausagins sausages
scarifyin' scare
screak squeak, scrape
scribblin's written matter, documents
serpent snake
shouldies shoulders
sicklee ill
skrike shriek
sky-dizzy afraid of heights
sky-like skylight
sky-savvy to know how to move around a roof safely
slew kill
slippins slippers
smincey little, small amount
sniff an odour
snitch nose
sockets socks
softlee quietly
somebiddy somebody, usually a woman
sorely painful

sorrowfill sorry
spewerpipe sewer
spookfill spooky
springly springy
squill squirrel
squish squash
step-in sister/brother substitute sister/brother
sunsit sunset
swede suede
sweetyheart girlfriend/boyfriend
swiftlee quickly
swollied swallowed

T

tastefill delicious
taytoos potatoes
thanklee thank you
thermoose thermos
thus that is why, therefore
tiddlypoles tadpoles
'tis it is
to-gathered together
trash and hide to disarrange a place and remove traces of habitation
travellin' be-foots walking

trove treasured junk
trubbil trouble
'twas it was
twigaloo musical instrument

U

uncool uncle
us we
usefil useful

V

veggibles vegetables
vessels pots etc
villins baddies

W

walligator alligator
welly well very well
whiff to detect a smell
whumperin' whimpering
whyfor why
windyfone gramophone

wobblin' wobbling
woe misery
Worldly War One WWI
Worldly War Two WWII
wringle mangle
wristit bracelet
wype to wipe

X

Y

yalp yelp
yay yes
yearnin' hoping
yesternights last night
yestertimes yesterday or
in the past
Yuletide Christmas-time
yonder over there
yourself you

Z

Don't miss the Goffins' other adventures!

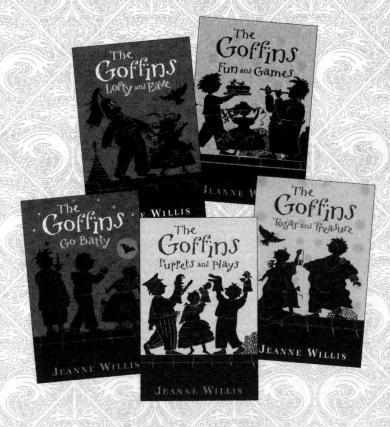

Is there a Goffin in *your* attic?